Bonded by Love

Malcolm's Story

By:K.Moore

This book is a work of fiction. Names, characters, businesses, organizations, places, events and incidents either are the product of the author's imagination or are used fictitiously. Any resemblance to actual persons, living or dead, events, or locales is entirely coincidental.

For more information, or to book an event, contact :
relatablefictionwriting@gmail.com
http://www.[1]relatablefictionwriting.com
Book design by Nakeia Davis
Cover design by Canva
ISBN-9798227157317
July 2024

Table of Contents

Dedication

Family is everything in every sense of the word. We may not like our family all the time but, we have to love them while we have them. As the eldest of your family you're the second in command after your parents. Your siblings look up to you for your guidance and leadership in life. Take pride in your role and shine bright in their eyes.

1

Introduction of Malcolm Rashad Williams

I'm Officer Malcolm Rashad Williams age(24) eldest child of Ezekiel(Zeek)Williams and Kahlani Coleman-Williams. I'm getting ready to marry the woman of my dreams, Kapri Smith. I hope to have a marriage like my parents because I've never seen my dad so happy as he was after meeting Ma. Anyone on the outside looking in could see that my biological mother Melody Stanton(deceased) broke his heart.

Growing up I never knew anything about my mother and thought my grandma was my mom throughout my childhood. Even the interactions of my dad and the mothers of my sister Harmony and my brother Christian were confusing for me growing up. Everytime I thought my dad had finally found love it ended with him having a broken heart.

By the time I got to high school Harmony came home talking about a new teacher at her school. The day dad picked us all up from school late was the best day ever. As a teenage boy I knew my dad was in love with my sister's teacher. Even I loved that woman from the moment we pulled up in front of the school. Christian leaned over to me in the backseat whispering " I think that's gonna be our mom forever".

Even Though I've only had Kahlani as a stepmom since the age of 14 she's the best mom any kid could ask for. Still to this day I can't believe the things my grandfather did to her throughout her life. Even now as an officer of the law I can't understand why anyone would want to harm my mom. In this story I'm going to show you my bond with the people that are near and dear to my heart.

2

Becoming a big brother the first time

2 months before my 4th birthday I became a brother to one of the most kind hearted people I've ever met. When dad brought her into the house I was a little confused. I knew Destiny had a baby in her belly but didn't the baby was out until the day after Harmony was born. My dad may think I wasn't paying attention but I was noticing that my dad was sad on that day.

Every night my dad would sit and read the bible to both of us until we both went to sleep. I even to this day sit with my fiance' at night and read the bible before bed. When it's our time to have a family we'll sit with our children and read bible stories to them. My dad was my hero even though he doesn't think of himself as one. Every night that my dad went to work and after Harmony went to sleep I'd ask my grandma to call my dad. I would ask my dad over the phone if I could be a policeman like him.

Every Time we'd call him my dad would tell me "You sure can son". I could tell as a toddler that my dad was smiling on the other end of the phone. Then he'd ask me what was Harmony doing while we were on the phone? We'd share a laugh as I told him "I gave her some warm milk and she went to sleep". After talking to my dad every night I'd watch my baby sister sleep until I passed out from exhaustion. While dad was out protecting us at work I was protecting my sister at home. Even when my grandma tried to put me in my bed I wanted to be close to the baby at all times.

Now that I think about it Destiny Richardson had me and my dad blinded when she was pregnant with my sister. But from that day it was up to me and dad to protect our household. My grandma Janette didn't know then but I was going to become an officer of the law just like my dad. She would always ask me "Mally why do you think you're the police after your daddy goes to work at night"? Grandma when daddy goes to work I'm the man of the house and a policeman in training, I responded.

For the next 3 years I watched my dad and grandma show me what it means to care for others. Letting me help and play with Harmony all the time helped build our bond. As siblings we talked about everything growing up. I felt it was my job to protect Harmony just as it was my dads' job to protect us. They say that the first woman a man loves is his mother but in my case the first woman I loved was my sister. We'll talk more about my relationship with Harmony later on in the story. Now I want to talk about the real MVP of our family Christian.

This guy is a little hard on himself about the kidnapping of himself and Camille. I am taking it hard as well but when you meet him you'll see how great of a kid he really is. Just like everyone says I'll make a great dad one day, I feel the same way about him as well.

3

Becoming a big brother a second time

By the time I was 7 and Harmony was 3 on March 6, 2007 we welcomed our brother Christian to the family. It made me feel like I was a dad at this point. After seeing how hard my dad worked to take care of 3 kids under the age of 10. Just think about it, he was 24 with 3 children and single. I hope I can be as great of a parent as my dad at some point in my life.

Now back to my main man Christian, we'll never tell him how Harmony and I used to argue over who would get to take care of him. Every two hours we'd play rock, paper, scissors to see who'd get to feed, change, burp and rock him to sleep. While dad was at work grandma would take us to the park and we'd argue over who'd get to push Christian on the swing. By the time we got home we'd get into an argument over who got to tell dad what happened at the park.

Grandma and dad would just stand there laughing at us then I'd let Harmony tell the story. I remember we went to the toy store and dad said that was the only place where Harmony and I could agree on anything. Mostly we only agreed on what toys to get for Christian first followed by our own toys. Which if you ask me now it was pointless because we played with Chistian's toys just to bond with him. Being in the second grade I was always worried about my siblings. I'd ask my dad if I could be homeschooled so I could be with Harmony and Christian all the time.

Dad would always say " You have to go make new friends, buddy". I'd look so confused then he'd be holding Christian and say " We'll always be your friends at home". Before I could start to cry Christian would start crying and I had to man up. Don't think I wasn't at school trying to figure out how to escape to go home. Because I was until the teacher distracted me with things I liked. Every art project or class assignment was dedicated to my family.

For anyone that reads the story of the Williams Family will understand the bond I have with my siblings. With the level of trauma our family has endured there is no way our bond could ever be weak. Throughout this story we'll talk about situations that brought us closer together as friends and family. Now let's get into the journey of my upbringing to become the man I am today.

It's a pretty sweet journey after seeing my dad endure so much in life. Until I met my PopPop, TuTu Kane, Uncle Max and Uncle Rashad my dad was my idol. I hope that the example that I set as a man will show Christian what man to be in life.

4

Finally getting a mother figure

By the time I was in Middle School at the age of 11 I asked my dad " Where is mommy "? My dad looked so sad when he turned to me and said "I don't know buddy" she used to be across the street with your grandparents. I didn't remember ever meeting them but dad said they came by all the time to see me. I guess I was more interested in Harmony and Christian to notice them.

By the time I was in High School and Harmony was in Middle School and Christian in Elementary in walks our mom Kahlani. That day dad picked us all up late due to his shift at the station. In front of the school there she was looking just like a mom hugging my sister. As they hugged, Harmony smiled in my direction which led to Christian leaning over to me saying " That's our stepmom, I can feel it".

The look on our dad's face made everything so clear to me and my siblings. I also learned that night that my dad was definitely a chick magnet and I hoped me and Christian didn't get that much attention.

But I could tell my dad never had to ask a girl out a day in his life because he was really nervous to ask Ma (Kahlani) out. He just sat there staring at her until Harmony told him to go talk to the woman. From what we could see from the car the two had an instant connection. To this day they both believe that Harmony was the one who set them up on their first date. What they don't know is after we got home me and my siblings got to planning their future together. After their first date we ambushed dad with questions before going to bed.

From the next week on Ma(Kahlani) started to bring Harmony home after school. Ma even made dinner for us and helped with our homework until dad got home. Shhh!!! don't tell anybody but we'd sneak out of our room and see dad and Ma on the porch kissing before she went home. I'd sit by dad's room and listen to him talk to Ma before going to bed. Watching their relationship shaped how I am with Kapri.

I'm not afraid to speak to Ma about anything that's on my heart. That woman was meant to be a mother her whole life. She always asked and answered questions, had her arms and heart open for anyone in need. The one thing that made me Love that woman was her Love and Knowledge of the Bible. My dad used to read the bible to us every night to get us to sleep, so having a mother figure who knew the bible strengthened our family.

Kahlani Marie Coleman-Williams is everything you'd ever want in a mother. No other woman on God's Green Earth could keep our family intact. And no other woman has been able to hold my dads heart in their hands like that woman. Ma is a strong woman that leads with heart and mind. When I was in school I looked for all her qualities in my future wife. I see Ma in Kapri everyday but I hope she's the good in herself that I see in her.

I'll ask Ma to go talk to Kapri at some point before our wedding. I feel it in my heart that Ma will make Kapri shine bright all the days of her life. I know I'll love both of those ladies all the days of my life from this moment on.

5

Life with Mom and Dad

Once my parents started dating, the atmosphere in our house was full of life. But the night they found out my grandfather had raped Ma it brought them closer as a couple. Hearing the sound of Ma crying that night broke our hearts and we wanted to make it better. The next morning my siblings and I asked our grandma if we could make Ma something to eat. When she opened her eyes and saw us in dad's room looking worried she smiled.

She was someone I could talk to about anything, I guess that was the teacher in her. No matter what question(s) I had Ma always had an answer.If she didn't have an answer she'd always say " let's get a second opinion from your dad"? Our mother/son relationship is just as strong as my relationship with my dad.

Even in high school Kahlani (Ma) would try to spend as much time with me and my siblings while dad wasn't home. Because once dad got home he wanted her all to himself. Ya know we never went to Kahlani's house other than the day we found out my grandpa was stalking her. I know I'm glad dad moved her in with us after that day. Ma was even kind enough to convince dad to let us be a part of both of their weddings.

It's like she could see how eager we were to be included in their union. Everytime I'd ask dad a question he'd have this twinkle in his eye and he'd always say "you gotta talk to Lani about that man". So I started going to Ma for answers to everything except how to be a man. I went to my dad, uncle Max and uncle Rashad about that.I also talked to PopPop and TuTu Kane(Jean) when they came to visit.

One thing I will say is after seeing the relationships between my parents, grandparents and my aunts/uncles. I know how to treat Kapri and what kind of foundation I want to lay down for my bride to be. Yeah

I said it I'm getting married to my College sweetheart but we'll talk more about that later on.

I hope to have a love story like the one I see my parents have everyday when I go next door to visit. My dad still to this very day leaves my mom scavenger hunt notes around the house every weekend. In the end Ma always has a smile on her face seeing us kids or my aunts and uncles waiting with open arms. When I first met Kapri the first thoughts that came to mind were "What scavenger hunt could I send her on"? "Let me ask dad what he would do for mom"?

Maybe I should ask PopPop what he'd do for grandma to keep the spark going. I might even ask uncle Max and uncle Rashad how they keep the spark going with my aunts. TuTu Kane is the best person to talk to when I want to make dinner for my sweet lady.

I may even sit down with uncle Max and uncle Rashad for relationship advice sometimes. Even Though their advice comes from my dad anyway. They'll make every bit of my life just as much fun as dad. Uncle Max is the most laid back guy I know on the force other than dad. Uncle Rashad is the most crazy person at the station while my grandma is the craziest person in my family.

It's unsettling for most people to not know the person who gave birth to them. But my dad made sure I was surrounded by women who would give me the love every child needs. Of course Ma, Aunt Cora and Aunt Regina are my favorite ladies to spend my childhood with. This blended family of mine will make you fall in Love every step of the way.

6

A grandma everyone can Love

Believe me that woman is a mess from start to finish and I don't know how PopPop puts up with her. You wouldn't think my dad is really her son because they're so different. I remember when dad told us he had to go check her about taking over his wedding to Ma. I couldn't believe that at all, I was sure she would've slapped my dad for that.

Once she sat down and told us how my grandfather treated her and my dad, I understood why she acts the way she does. I'm sure you've read about my grandma's dating life in the other books and are still laughing with the rest of us. At the hospital when Ma told me and Harmony about grandma's dates, I swore I'd never bring a girl home while she's at the house.

The day I met Kapri was the best day ever until I got home and grandma was there. Before I could sit down she started firing off the questions about Kapri. I looked over at my dad who was shaking his head saying "she did the same thing to me when I met your biological mother". I know she didn't mean any harm but couldn't you say hello to a brotha before starting the interrogation of my love life?

The day I finally got the courage to bring Kapri to meet the family grandma was ready to start her interrogation of Kapri. But thank God PopPop was there to distract her but then my sister did the questioning along with Ma. But knowing Janette she will not be out done by anyone, so every holiday she makes sure to act up at all costs. Just wait til I tell you how she asks at my wedding.

Then there's TuTu Wahine(Ramona) is the coolest grandma anyone could ask for. I see where Ma gets her temperament from when the two are in the room together. After hearing the story of what she and Ma endured at the hands of Marcus Coleman it tugs at your heartstrings. She deserves all the hugs in the world so everytime I see her the first thing I do is wrap her in a big bear hug. I know it's hard for TuTu Wahine to keep a straight face when she has a comedic friend like Janette.

I'm sure you all remember our Holiday dinner before their wedding when Janette couldn't identify half the food at the table. It was hard for all of us, especially Ma and TuTu Wahine to not laugh as they explained what we were eating. I know TuTu Wahine was stressed out when Janette pretty much demanded that TuTu Kane make all the food for their double wedding. We all know she meant well but she was and is just too extra for most people.

I still can't get over how she acted on her honeymoon with PopPop. I told dad that maybe grandma should've become a cop instead of us. For a 60 yr old woman to instill fear in a person to the point of confessing to a crime, she'd make a better cop than any of us on the force. It's hard to believe PopPop has police training and grandma doesn't at all. The way she grills people lets you know which one of them is the good cop and who is the bad cop in their house.

At times we wish Janette would be as laid back as Ramona but then you realize how boring it would be if they were both the same. So we have to Love them just the way they are and that's just what I plan to do. Now let's talk about those 4 adorable siblings of mine: Camille, Brandon, Ann Marie Williams and Serenity Reynolds.

These little people have stolen my heart just like Harmony and Christian did at birth. How do you not fall in Love with the innocence of those who look up to you? As their big brother I try to give them as much of my attention as humanly possible. There's not a day that goes by that I don't worry about their safety.

Here I am sounding like a dad but in a since I am when it comes to all of my siblings. My dad just shakes his head when I show up at the station asking questions about my siblings. He likes to say "Son you live right next door to visit them" you don't have to ask me everyday.

Then he'll say " you also live across the street from the baby, just go over to see her". I understand where my dad is coming from and I'll be doing that a lot. But like I said I'll describe the bond I have with my 4 younger siblings. And don't get me wrong I Love Harmony and Christian just as much. I've gone through these young years with them and enjoyed them to the fullest.

I pretty much played daddy to Harmony and Christian while our dad was at work. I'm sure grandma Jannete didn't know what to do with me wanting to take care of them myself. To think I tried to skip school to take care of my siblings. Now I'd love to take as much time off to be with the younger ones.

7

4 pieces of my heart

When Camille was born I felt like I was looking at Harmony all over again.Watching her grow up is a highlight in my life along with Brandon and Ann Marie. When Camille and Christian were kidnapped by me and Harmony's mothers it made the love I have for them stronger. My willingness to protect my siblings will never change for the world. Even when I become a parent one day I'll continue to look out for them.

Now little Serenity is a piece of my mom (Melody) that I will cherish. I never had a bond with Melody like the one I have with Kahlani but Serenity is innocent and deserves to know I Love her. Since she's right across the street with my mom's parents, I go over there often to hang out with them. I even buy stuff for her when I'm out buying things for Camille and the twins. Kapri always says that I'll be a great father one day after I come from the store with lots of bags.

To tell you the truth I feel like a dad everytime I see their faces light up as I walk into the house. Especially baby Serenity when I feed her a bottle while talking to my grandparents. As a man I feel that Jehovah God made this my mission to be a big brother to all these innocent, great, kindhearted souls in my family. Just as Jesus did for all of us when he gave his life for all of us.

Everyday as an officer of the law I put my life on the line alongside my dad and uncles for our families. I'm glad Kapri and I live next door but Camille might give our parents a heart attack by sneaking out the house to come see me and Kapri every weekend. I do take her across the street to bond with Serenity when I go to drop off supplies for her. I think Camille just loves babies overall, it doesn't matter if it's the twins or Serenity she wants to help.

I told Kapri that when we decide to have kids there is a live-in babysitter next door. Camille asks us every weekend if we decided to have a baby yet because she wants to make some money. Believe me when I say no matter what my sister does in the future she'll get paid. I hope she follows in Ma's footsteps into education since she loves babies so much. I'll ask my grandparents if Camille can help out with Serenity, Kapri and I will pay her too.

8

Present Day

Here we are on Aug 2, 2023 having breakfast in the kitchen of our home. Kapri looks at me worried and I don't like when she looks like that. Baby why are you looking at me like that? What's on your mind? talk to your man. Well Bae, what if the Chief is trying to ruin your career, Kapri asked concerned. Baby his beef is with my dad and uncles besides I was a toddler back then it's not my issue. Okay Babe I'll leave it alone but if he comes around here and botters me, it's gonna be a problem, she said.

I know my woman and I know when she's serious about a topic. After being in a Psychology Class with her for 3 months there will be no arguing with her about this issue. Because I love her I simply said" I'll keep my eyes and ears open" if the chief is up to no good dad and I will take care of it. While you take care of that I'll be next door with Ma working on this wedding planning, then she gave me a kiss and headed for the door.

I made my way to the station where my dad and uncles were just arriving at the same time. We all embraced one another before asking me how the wedding planning was going? Snickering, I looked down saying " she's with Ma and the girls planning right now" all I'm worried about is how much overtime I'll need to pay for the wedding. They all laughed remembering all the hours they worked to pay for their weddings.

Walking into the station we were met by the Chief talking to Sandy the disbatcher. Upon noticing the 4 of us walking in Chief Wilkenson approached us with a sinister smile on his face. That made me wonder if everything Kapri said at the house was really a cause for alarm. Then he handed me a box saying " Congrats on the engagement". I opened the box which had a flyer for a dating site.

Seeing the flyer uncle Max tore it up yelling "No way Chief, you're not going to traumatize this man the way you traumatized us". Neither of us could enjoy our honeymoon because your blind dates from that site were stalking us the whole time, Rashad said with contempt. There is no way I'll allow you to harass my son with these ridiculous pranks Chief, is this why you were at my house 3 months ago, Zeek asked noticeably irritated? With a smirk the Chief replied, Yeah I was trying to bring some humor to your family after all the craziness you've been through, sorry if I upset you.

In shock I now have to go home and tell Kapri it was all just a joke all along. The Chief just thought we were stressed out from all the drama with people trying to harm my mom and siblings.

For some the Chief's joke could be thought of as insensitive but for me it was laughable. The reaction of my dad was extremely serious and no laughing matter. I understand how he feels and I would react the same way about my child. Hopefully when I have a child nobody tries me like that for my family's safety. My family is everything to me and nobody will ever change that.

9

Joint Bachelor/Bachelorette Party

On Friday September 13, 2023 uncle Max showed up with a huge party bus. I went out first to take a look around and the first person to catch my eye was my mom. She ran past me and into the house to get Kapri. On the way down the street Kapri asked me what was going on tonight. All I could do was shake my head in confusion looking over to uncle Max.

Nephew tonight is a couple's night and your joint Bachelor/Bachelorette party. The rest of the girls are at the event space waiting for us to deliver the bride and groom. Kapri started tearing up at the news of the night being all about us. As we pulled up to The RichKick dance Studio I was confused but my bride was overjoyed so that made me relax. As we entered the door our entire group was there (1)Uncle Rashad and Aunt Regina (2) Dametrius and Jazzlene (3) Travion and Harmony (4) PopPop and Grandma Janette (5) TuTu Kane and TuTu Wahine. Aunt Cora and my parents shouted surprise as we looked around in amazement.

Grandson since your bride loves to dance and majored in dance at school your mom thought we should take y'all dancing instead of to the strip club, Janette announced. Yes; son your bride said the one dance she didn't get to learn and that's the Waltz, Kahlani said with a warm smile. And we're all going to learn it with you and perform it with you infront of all your wedding guests, Harmony stated while hugging her big brother.

5 minutes later the instructors Jesse and Bianca entered the room excited to teach this group. Each of the men admitted to not being the best dancers in the room. But for the ladies they would each try just to see them smile. After 2 hours the class was over and TuTu Kane and TuTu Wahine did the best out of all the couples. Walking over to Kapri and

myself Jesse stated; you guys should take lessons from your grandparents since they mastered the dance.

Then we all went to dinner at our favorite place, World Tavern. During dinner questions were coming from everyone at the table about the wedding. Starting with my mom asking what's the date of the wedding, followed by Aunt Cora asking what the colors for the wedding were. Then Aunt Regina asked what venue we chose to have the wedding at. Grandma Janette asked Kapri about dress shopping and the room got real quiet. We all know how my grandma is in dress shops and the spotlight isn't on her.

No Ma'am I haven't picked my dress yet, I am waiting for my mom to come back from Jamaica first. She's taking care of my grandparents right now. My grandpa just had back surgery and my grandma had a stroke trying to take care of my grandpa. She told me this morning in a zoom call that she should be back by Thanksgiving so I'll go shopping the first week of December. As for everything else we haven't looked at venues yet but I do want a Spring Wedding, and the date is April 25, 2024

Now that y'all know all about our wedding, Sis when are you and Travion jumping the broom, I asked? Well Bro since you asked ours will be the same year as yours but on December 25th Harmony said happily. So my sister and I will be getting wed 8 months apart next year. Now that everyone had full bellies and all the information on both weddings it was time to go home. As we entered our home after saying goodnight to everyone Kapri just shook her head.

What's wrong? I asked concerned , taking her by the hand and heading for the couch. I don't know how it's gonna go having your grandma and my Jamaican mother in the same dress shop together. They seem so much alike that I'm afraid of being embarrassed, Kapri expressed. Baby all you can do is try being in the same room with the two of them, and just hope they'll behave themselves. Mal I truly hope so because Jamaicans can be very critical people. After our talk we went to bed for the night, sweet dreams my princess.

That night I prayed that Kapri had a great time out with the ladies. I understand her reservations because I'm worried about what might fly out of the mouth of my grandma Janette. That woman can be hilarious and at other times she can be insensitive to others.

<h1 style="text-align:center">10</h1>

<h1 style="text-align:center">Wedding Prep activities</h1>

4 weeks later on October 13,2023 Kapri and I took Camille and Serenity with us to look at some venues. The first venue was The LakeShore Villas on an Indian Reservation on the outskirts of Richfield. As we walked around I could tell it was more of a honeymoon space than a wedding location so we left there. The next spot to check out was a castle on the hill on Cormell Ridge Lake. As soon as we stepped in all of the girls were speechless at the massiveness even Serenity just looked around which made me smile.

After the tours we took the kids to eat and while Kapri was changing Serenity's diaper I asked for Camille's opinion of the two places. Camille was very serious when she told me " I like the castle but I think we should look at one more place before choosing it". I couldn't agree more with my little sister on this one. Once Kapri came back with Serenity I told her what Camille said and she also agreed we should look at one more place.

After lunch I took my girls to see the final place on my list which was The Hyatt Regency Hotel on Desert Creek Beach. Sitting in the hills overlooking the Tennessee Skyline with a 10 minute walk to the sandy beach area. Upon walking into the lobby each of the girls looked around then looked at me uninterested. Then Kapri leaned over whispering in my ear " I think this place would be better suited for Harmony's wedding not ours". I agreed with them so it's settled we'll be getting married on Cormell Ridge Lake in the castle on the hill.

Once we got home and dropped Serenity off at my grandparents home across the street we could hear Camille shouting about how she couldn't wait for the wedding. All we could do was laugh at that child, I love that kid. By October 25, 2023 my mom had taken us to meet with caterers and decorators for the wedding. I almost thought my mom was trying to recreate her wedding to my dad through us. Her excitement was just as amplified as Camille's to see this wedding dream come true. By November 1, 2023 my soon to be mother in law came to visit us.

Kapri was so happy to see her mom but apprehensive about her hanging with my grandmother Janette. On Friday November 15, 2023 the girls went dress shopping and boy was it something to talk about. From the moment the ladies stepped into the shop Kapri's mom Janice and my grandma Janette were off to the races with their critiques of everything. My princess had to ask my mom how she was able to deal with my grandma in public. Camille walked over and told her " Don't worry about grandma I'll deal with her for ya". That's all it took for Kapri to go along with the task.

11

Dress shop fairytale

The saleswoman came to greet them with drinks and took Kapri to pick out dresses to try on. When they returned Janice and Janette started with their critique of the dresses. Dress(1) was a Sophisticated fit and flare has a sheer bodice with beaded floral embroidered lace and keyhole back. Both Janice and my mom started to tear up. Janette and Camille were speechless at the sight. So this is a contender, the saleswoman said with a smile. Dress(2) was a Gorgeous fit and flare with a sweetheart neckline with frosted, textured floral embroidery and a chic Larissa satin overskirt for added drama.

Now Janette had something to say so all the ladies braced themselves for it. Baby that dress is nice but it makes you look like you're stealing someone else's man not snagging your own. The room was silent for what seemed like forever until my mom and Camille started laughing. Well let's try on our next dress shall we, the saleswoman said with a smile. Dress(3) was a Lace Fit and Flare with Beaded Appliqués Accented with 3D Flowers. Janice sat straight up saying: Put that dress back now, you look like a plucked chicken from the farm and Janette started laughing and rolling around on the floor.

At this point Kapri turned to the saleswoman and replied: let's take a look at the final dress. Back in the dressing room Kapri stepped into the Full tulle ball gown, ruching in the bodice and a sweetheart neckline. Paired with a layered tulle cathedral veil. This time Camille was first to speak saying: you look like a princess but I still love the first dress. So Kapri took a vote with all the ladies

By a show of hands how many love dress (1) and all the ladies raised their hands even Ann Marie. Ok now how many like dress (2) and no one raised their hand. The same went for dress(3) in the vote for the dresses. Now how many like dress (4) and all the ladies raised their hands again. So we have a tie. I don't know which one to get, Kapri said sadly looking over to the saleswoman. Well young lady you're in luck because both of these dresses are on clearance so you could buy them both today. Dress (1) is on sale for $500 and Dress (4) is on sale for $1500 and with your budget of $3000 you'll save $1000.

That's a great deal, daughter Janice said, embracing Kapri with a hug. Just wear the ballgown for the ceremony and the first dress for the reception. When Kapri came home and told me all about her day with the ladies I couldn't do anything but smile. I'm glad our families are getting along well and there's no drama to derail our big day. Then my little sister rang the doorbell full of joy. She wanted to tell me how much fun it was to go shopping with the girls. And they even got a pretty dress for Serenity and Ann Marie to wear for the wedding.

12

Men's Shopping Day

Now on November 29.2023 all the men went to Men's Warehouse to pick out our suits. I chose to go with a traditional Black Suit for the wedding. The rest of the guys chose White suits with black lapels. Once we were done there it was time to have some food and head home. So we went to Sideline Diner for a quick bite. Just as we were about to leave, PopPop motioned to a table of ladies trying to get our attention.

My dad just shook his head saying this is crazy. At first women were outside of buildings flirting with me when I was engaged. Now they're in groups flirting with my son who's getting married. Then he looked over at me saying: now Kapri will have to deal with all the haters just like your mom does when we go out. I looked around the table replying: Just like you guys I know what woman has my heart and attention. Just to be clear it's none of these women here or out there.

I'm glad to hear you say that son, my dad replied. I said the same thing about your mom and stood by my word ever since. Yeah, nephew, your aunt Cora is the only woman to hold my attention along with the triplets. No other woman can get me to abandon my home, uncle Max replied. Now that your aunt Regina is pregnant I know I'm stuck with her for the long haul, uncle Rashad said with a chuckle.

Once I made my way home Kapri was sitting in the living room wrapped in a blanket. Why aren't you in bed beautiful? I asked worriedly. I couldn't sleep in there without you, she answered. I picked her up in my arms and carried my bride upstairs to our bed. The next day at the station I asked my dad if my mom stayed up waiting for him to come home at night. With a shy smile he replied "Yeah but she wasn't worried about me, she had bad nightmares of your grandfather abusing her as a child". The only way she could sleep was when I was home with you guys then she felt safe.

Hearing my father tell me this made me feel bad for Ma and now I need to talk to Kapri to see what's keeping her up when I'm not home. Before we went over to my parents' for Thanksgiving I sat Kapri on the couch and asked "What's bothering you baby"? Apprehensively Kapri replied " I'm just scared of being alone, I'm an only child and with my dad not being in my life growing up I'm just scared all the time". Now knowing this hurt my heart and all I could say was " Baby just go next door if I'm not home and you get scared" My mom and dad are only children as well just go talk to them next door.

13

Thanksgiving shenanigans

Once we walked into my parents' home I explained to them how Kapri was feeling. My dad turned sad eyes to Kapri and reached out his hand for her to take. After taking my dads' hand he told her " Kapri, you're going to be my daughter in 6 months when you marry my son, so don't be afraid to call me dad or talk to me about anything".

Just as they finished getting Kapri comfortable in walked Janette and PopPop. PopPop was laughing at grandma and she was complaining as usual about some woman trying to get with Pop. Ma!!! What are you complaining about now, my dad asked? Since you must know what Mike was laughing at, I'll tell you. While we were at the store to pick up our dinner last night the cashier decided to slip him her number right in front of me. I'm not mad that he gave it back to her and turned to leave the store. I'm mad that she put it back into the bag like I wasn't going to find it.

When we got home to eat I found the heifers number in the bag and told him we're going to stop over there on our way here tonight. And that's what we did, I just wanted to explain that she was out of line to do what she did. This chick decided to choose violence and swing at me so I whooped her behind in front of everyone. But the funny part was when I started whooping her butt and the girl ignored me and started taking her clothes off to give all the men a striptease and the girl had some Depends on. Then she got so scared that she pooped herself and it started running out on the floor so I ran out to the car.

That's why your PopPop is so tickled with laughter all the way here. By the time grandma was done telling the story we were all in a fit of laughter just as Harmony and Travion arrived. Grandma told them the story, making us laugh all over again. Then we sat down as a family and had dinner before going home for the night. Back at our home Kapri looked over at me in bed and told me she felt like family after being around my family.

The next day Harmony called asking for details on the wedding to which I asked about hers. My sister told me she was struggling with wedding planning so I told her to check out the places we didn't like to see if one of them matches her theme. Then I told her if she wanted to know anything about our wedding just ask Camille because she picked out everything for us. In shock Harmony shouted " I think my little sister should be my wedding planner too". All Kapri and I could do was laugh at the sound of that and tell her Camille would love that.

Sis I think she would love to do just that for her big sister like she did for me. Hey; sis Camille will be asking to babysit your future children, just so you know. Harmony replied, I'll be on the lookout for the baby conversation with a chuckle. We then said our goodbyes and went to bed for some rest.

14

End of one year/Start of another

On December 13th my bride turned 23 and my family wanted to celebrate her for the day. My mom took her and Janice to the spa for some girl talk. Of course they had to tell Janice about what my grandma did on Thanksgiving. After their spa treatment the moms' took Kapri to meet with a caterer to sample food for the reception. Kapri was apprehensive since I wasn't there to sample the food and give my opinion. When she came home the first thing she said was " we're going to meet with the caterer to try the food again". Okay, was all I could think to say just to calm her down.

By the 25th we again went next door to be with the family before going home. Y'all know my grandma is always going to be extra anytime our family gets together. So of course Janette got into some more trouble that left PopPop laughing again at his wife. Now grandma got into an altercation at the mall over a toy for Brandon and Ann Marie. She claims the lady tried to steal the toy from her cart and slapped her. Then as she put it " we started throwing hands in the middle of the floor".

Now grandma you know you're too old to be fighting people over a toy. Just let Jesus guide you to turn the over cheek in the situation. My grandma told us if she turned the other cheek and the girl had hit her again and I quote " I'd be stomping her out in the parking lot all the way to the police station". My poor dad was sitting at the head of the table shaking his head along with PopPop.

I looked at Kapri and asked are you sure you want to marry into this comedy show of a family? That beauty nodded her head and continued to laugh at my grandma. Y'all don't know how happy I am that she still wants to marry me. After dessert everyone said goodnight and went their separate ways. On December 31st Kapri and I spent the whole day together since it was my day off. I also wanted to show her she had nothing to fear with me in her life.

I even called TuTu Kane and TuTu Wahine to talk to her and make her feel welcome in our family. Other than mom and dad these two are the best people to speak to for relationship advice in my opinion. Then TuTu Wahine gave us an idea to come to Hawaii for our honeymoon to hang out with them for 2 weeks. Kapri's face lit up like a star at night with excitement hearing the idea. So I guess once we meet with the caterer we'll be all set for the wedding.

15

New Year/ new Us

Welcome to 2024 Y'all we are 120 days away from our big day. I know Kapri is nervous because I sure am but can't show it. I guess it's showing on my face because my dad and uncles ask me at the station every other day if I 'm Ok. I tell everyone that I am but they know I'm lying and going crazy. My dad and uncles took me to the sports bar to watch some Monday night football to relax.

Man I can't wait for this wedding to be complete so I can be alone with my lady. I said more to myself than anyone else. I hear you son. I said the same thing when I married your mom both times, my dad said with a smile.Dad was it really this stressful to marry the girl of your dreams? Yeah; son but I never let her or you kids know I was sweating bullets leading up to both of those weddings. But when they were both over I was so relieved and could finally breathe a sigh of relief.

I have 3 ½ months until I can have that relief so I hope Kapri will take it easy on me. Once we got home my mom was at the house with Kapri who was crying.Mom what happened why is she crying? Son she had a bad dream and called me over. I was just telling her that nothing will go wrong on her wedding day. Thanks for coming over to be with her. I'll take it from here. You guys have a goodnight.

Once we were alone I held Kapri in my arms and kissed the top of her head. Baby I'm right here and I promise your wedding will be perfect and that's my word. She nodded her head and asked me to carry her to our bed upstairs. As her man I did just that and held her for the rest of the night.

By February 1st Kapri and I went to meet with three different caterers and decided on Callie's Soul Food Express. We were even given samples of the food to take home and share with the family. Now that we had taken care of all the big wedding topics all we had to do was pick the DJ and Decorator. But now my aunts and uncles are saying they'll take care of that for us. On February 10th my aunt Cora and aunt Regina along with my mom took Kapri to meet with some Party Decorators. Out of all four Kapri chose Mindy Lesley, an up and coming Wedding Planner in Richfield.

Kapri came home filled with joy after her day out with the ladies. She told me I'd love the design of our wedding as much as she does. Anything my baby chooses I will love, after all she chose to spend the rest of her life as my Queen. It will make me proud just standing there to hear her vows in front of our family and friends.

16

My Favorite Valentine

On February 13, 2024 Kapri had gone to bed early so I took the time to set up a scavenger hunt for my fiance'. While she was asleep I placed several notes around the house and one in her car for her to find. The next morning while i was sleeping she found note(**1**)on her mirror stating:

To my Princess

In this mirror I hope you see yourself as the beauty that stole my heart 3 years ago. In the top drawer is a token of my affection that reminds me of you and I.

Malcolm

In the top drawer was a black box with a pink ribbon around it. Upon opening the box Kapri was shocked to find a gold locket with a picture of the two of them from their first date. On the underside of the box was another note telling Kapri to go into her closet. In the closet was another note on the wall under the light switch saying:

My Bride to be

Take a walk to the back of your closet and look up on the shelf. The bag is Blue with a lovely gift for you. A gift that will make your feet sway on our wedding day.

Malcolm

In the bag was a pair of White diamond studded Alex Mcleod Strappy Heeled Sandals. Kapri was on her knees in tears of joy at how I felt about her. As she was putting the box down she noticed another note telling her I left something for her in her car when she leaves for work that morning. So after making breakfast Kapri headed for the door making her way to Starlight Salon where she was a Hair Stylist.

Before she could leave there was a note on the steering wheel that went as follows:

Hey Beautiful

In the glove compartment is another clue to our night on this Valentine's Day. Enjoy your day at work and I'll see you tonight.You'll always shine bright at Starlight on any day or night in my eyes.

Your Prince Charming:Malcolm

Kapri opened the glove box and found a sheet of paper with another note stating:

When you get home there will be more scavenger hunt notes starting in the garage. Once you find the last note is when our date night will begin. Don't try going back inside to find out what's in store tonight because I haven't set it up yet. Have a good day baby

Luv U with all my heart

Malcolm

Now with Kapri off to work it was time for me to get up and find something to eat. Just as I was getting out of bed there was a surprise for me as well. On the nightstand by the bed was a tray of heart-shaped pancakes with sausage patties and scrambled eggs along with Cranberry Juice and a note:

Morning Handsome

Just as you have nourished my soul with your charm and kind heart I decided to do the same for you. I made you a meal fit for a king(My) King. This isn't our first Valentine's Day together but I wanted you to know what's in store for the future. When we become 1 in 2 ½ months from now.

Kapri

That literally took my breath away to know what's in her heart. After I finished my breakfast and took a shower I stepped into my closet only to find another gift from my bride to be. On the floor was a white box with a note that read:

Prince Charming

This is for you ,I was going to give this to you the night before our wedding but here you go. Another item to add to your charming style

that attracted me to you. I look forward to seeing you wear these on our wedding day.

Your Princess

Kapri

In the box was a pair of Black FairWether Diamond encrusted leather loafers. Choosing to marry this woman was the best choice I 've ever made in my life. After seeing this act of love from my baby I got dressed and finished setting out my other notes for Kapri. Then it was off to work for the day. When I arrived at the station dad and my uncles were in a conversation about date night with the ladies.

After I greeted them my dad asked what I had planned for the night? I explained that Kapri wanted to stay in but I set up a scavenger hunt to lure her out of the house. To which uncle Max excitedly said: come out with us tonight I know the girls will love to have Kapri with them tonight. Then I thought about those notes I left her at home for the night and smiled saying: I think that's a great plan unc. We went on with our day but I wondered what Kapri's face would look like when she saw me waiting outside to take her on our date.

Later on that night.......

Kapri got off work at 4:30 and arrived home at 5pm pulling into the 2-car garage. On the entry door to the house was a note saying:

Hey Baby

Head upstairs and see what I left for you on the bed. After you take a rest I want you to get dressed. We're going somewhere special that I think you'll like. I'll be home by 7:30 to pick you up alright

Malcolm

Kapri didn't hesitate making her way into the house and up the stairs. In the doorway of their room Kapri stood in shock at the sight before her on the bed. A burnt orange silk blouse with a black faux fur jacket along with black wool pants and black wedge heels. Oh how I love that man; she thought as she laid down for a quick nap. After setting her alarm she was awakened at 7pm to get ready for her date.

After a quick shower Kapri was dressed in no time at all and waiting for Malcolm on the couch. Right on time at 7:30 Malcolm walked into the front door with that charming smile she loved so much. With his hand extended Malcolm asked Kapri if she was ready to go? Once in the car Kapri asked "Where are we going tonight babe"? We're going on a group date with all the people we love, I told her before pulling off into the night.

As we drove across town I could tell Kapri wanted to ask more questions.I'd gladly answer any question she had about the night but all she did was stare at me the whole drive. When we arrived at the Karaoke bar my baby lit up with joy not knowing who was in there waiting for us. As the door opened my mom came running up to us with her arms wide for a hug. With everyone greeted it was time to have some fun on stage.

17

Sweet Karaoke Lullabies

We let the ladies choose their songs first starting with Aunt Regina performing the classic "Love No Limit" by the Queen of HipHop Soul. Uncle Rashad was beaming with pride at his 8 ½ month pregnant wife having the time of her life. I hope to see Kapri that happy and full of life when we start a family.Next Aunt Cora chose a Chaka Khan classic "Sweet Thang" followed by my mom singing "Your Smile" by Angela Winbush.

Lastly my baby performed a favorite song of hers "Rather Be" by H.E.R. Then it was up to the men to perform next and after the standing ovation how can you follow that? But we gave it a try belting out a Temptations classic "My Girl". Every woman in the building was falling in Love with us 4 black men. But the only women we were concerned with are the women we came here with. After the standing ovation we received, all 4 couples went to have dinner and headed home.

Later that night I turned to Kapri in bed and asked her what she thought about our date night. The smile on her face was all I needed to know she had a great time. I know she'll fit right in with the Williams family. Man, I can't wait to marry this woman. By the 28th of the month all we could do was wait it out. Everyday was making me more nervous by the second but excited nonetheless.

On March 1st Janice came to stay with us until the wedding which was good for Kapri. Knowing she wasn't feeling alone while I'm at work everyday. I know you may think we're both crazy for working up until our wedding day. But just so you know Kapri only worked until the end of March. I only worked until 2 weeks before the wedding, that's enough time for me to relax before the big day. Seeing the bond of love between mother and daughter made my heart glad.

By April 1st Kapri was worried that something would go wrong regarding our wedding. It took a lot of hugs and prayer that day to keep her calm. By 11pm that night she finally calmed down and went to sleep. I was so relieved at that point and settled in for a good night's sleep. Then at 6am I was awakened by my future mother-in-law asking for my opinion on something she wants to do for the wedding. Janice let me know that since Kapri's dad wasn't in the picture, she'd be walking her daughter down the aisle at the wedding. Janice also let me know she would be making the wedding cake for us.

That will be a blessing to my pockets when it comes to paying for this wedding . If we could cut any other corners that would be great too . Maybe I'll even ask Janice if she could include some Jamaican Cuisine in our reception for us .

18

Start of Happily ever after

The week of our wedding has arrived and I'm so ready to see my bride at the altar. On April 20th our families went with us to Cormell Ridge Lake to relax leading up to the wedding. The castle had several wings with the kitchen and a formal dining room were held. An elevator was in the center of the foyer leading to the rooms upstairs. The second level housed the chapel and ballroom. On the third level is where we stayed with our guests.

In the west wing overlooking the front garden is where all the ladies resided for the week. Over in the east wing me and the fellas got settled in for the week ahead. After everyone was comfortable, a worker at the castle let us know there was also a Game Room and Theater on the main level that we didn't notice upon arrival. We let the kids watch a movie while the adults went into the game room across the hall. To our surprise Serenity slept through the movie. After dinner we all parted ways and went to bed except for Serenity who wanted her big brother. I took her back to my room where my dad gave me a crash course in parenting 101 throughout the night.

The next morning after breakfast I gave Serenity back to my mom and my little sister wasn't happy about that. Kapri walked over and gave me a hug and whispered in my ear " you'll make a great dad one day, I can tell". Then we made our way outside for some activities. **Activity(1) Wedding Scrabble and a Matching Game** adults on the left and kids on the right. After the ladies beat the men in scrabble they went over to play the matching game with the kids.

Then it was time for lunch in the gazebo where everyone laughed together as a family. All the kids were still amped up at dinner time for more fun. So Kapri took them into the game room to play before bed. Once everyone was ready for bed and we went to our separate wings I couldn't sleep at all so I sent a text to my bride.

Malcolm-Hey baby; I had a great time today and I hope you did as well. Sweet dreams my princess see you in the morning.

Kapri- HI handsome: I also had a great time today just as you did. Sleep well prince charming I'll see you in the morning as well.

Next day, April 21st after breakfast it was time for more family fun activities. This time we played tug of war with the kids along with all the men playing dominos on the lawn. The best part was that Camille rubbed in the face of all the men as she was the strongest of all the ladies. That 8 yr old has my heart in a chokehold with all her sassy cuteness. I'm so proud to be her big brother watching her grow up. The reminder of her kidnapping still bothers me at times but my sessions with Dr.Matthews have been helping. After another fun family day it was time to rest and see what's in store for tomorrow.

Day(3) April 22nd the adults played twister in the grassy lawn while the kids played bean bag toss. Then a game of simon says was played by the entire family. Guys with 72 hrs until I say I Do there really isn't any nervousness on my part. But I did notice that Kapri was getting over anxious today while we were outside when the staff kept asking her if she was ready. When we get to our rooms tonight I'll ease her worries because she has nothing to fear leading up to our big day. Once everyone including Serenity was in bed for the night I left a text for Kapri to help her relax for the night.

Malcolm- Baby I noticed you were getting overwhelmed today. Here's some comfort for you sweet dreams Baby. **Matthew 6:34**

Alone in her two bedroom suite Kapri read the text with a faint smile on her lips. Her mom Janice was in the next room sound asleep so Kapri opened her Bible on her phone to read the scripture. After reading the scripture 3 times Kapri text me before going to sleep.

Kapri- Thank You for that encouraging word babe. I can rest now. Good night Handsome.

Day (4) April 23rd we did arts and crafts with the kids on the lawn. It warmed my heart to see Kapri smiling while finger painting with Serenity. Those two teeth Serenity tugged at my heartstrings knowing she was about to turn 2 in February 2025. Time is moving fast watching my siblings grow up before my eyes. We also played ring toss with the little people in the grass before lunch. During lunch Grandma Stanton asked where Kapri and I planned to go for our honeymoon?

I explained that we were going to spend a week with her mom in Jamaica and then we'd spend a week in Hawaii with TuTu Kane and TuTu Wahine. I could tell my response made my mom's heart glad by her tears. Then Grandpa Stanton took Kapri by the hand stating: We know Malcolm's mother (our daughter Melody) wasn't a mother to him at all. But we have been close to his dad his whole life and we welcome you as our granddaughter. You can come across the street to talk at any time.

This moment was monumental to both of us and all of the ladies were in tears at this point. Next Grandma Stanton followed by all the other ladies came to our table to give Kapri a hug.Camille and Ann Marie held on a little longer than the other ladies to whisper " Your as much our sister as Harmony is OK sis".

With a teary smile Kapri replied "OK sis" making everyone around them laugh as well. At the end of the day I looked myself in the mirror saying "you can make it 48 hrs to see her at the altar". It's time for me to join the rest of my family and have some sweet dreams. After saying my prayers to the creator of all things I was out like a light.

It's now 24 hrs until "I Do" and honestly I can't wait until tomorrow. On this day all the ladies went out on a shopping trip while the fellas went to the gym and arcade. It amazed me to see my granddad's play basketball with the energy of someone my age. Christian and Brandon play video games at home together because I didn't understand anything they did in the arcade.

They made me feel really old but just like anything else I come across in life " I'm a student of the game". Meanwhile in the shopping mall the girls were playing dress up in every store. Kapri got the royal treatment from all the shopkeepers as all of her elders told stories of their wedding day. Even some of the shopkeepers told stories of their marriages. When the girls returned from their day out they all looked refreshed and vibrant.

They all raved about going to the spa and getting their nails done. They think we didn't notice all the bags being brought in by the staff when they arrived but all the fellas saw them. It's a good thing we each have houses with enough space to accommodate our woman's stuff.

19

The fairytale begins here

Finally April 25, 2024 has arrived and I feel like a new man today y'all. Bro. Swanson will be officiating our wedding and he along with some of our Richfield Congregation will be arriving in a few hours. The day I introduced Kapri to my family was also the day my mom aided Kapri in understanding bible truths. We studied with my parents every week leading to the day I proposed.

Somehow today feels so majestic to me as I awake from my slumber. I'm not anxious about anything and can't wait to see the dress Kapri raved about months ago. The staff at the castle had a barber come in to take care of us men but my dad told them they weren't needed. That's because our personal barber was invited to the wedding and agreed to take care of us as a wedding gift to me. Once all the guys were groomed to the nines it was time to get dressed.

Across the way my bride and all the ladies were getting their hair and nails done in their rooms. Camille shot me a text of Serenity, AnnMarie and herself in their dresses while they were getting ready. I showed the text to my dad who smiled and asked me to send the photo to his phone. With the temp being a comfortable 75 degrees all the fellas hopped on the elevator to go outside for the ceremony.

At 1:30pm we were all lined up talking to the other guests as we awaited the arrival of the ladies. Bro. Swanson was already outside greeting the other members of the congregation when we got into our places. At 1:45 the processional started with Ma, Harmony, Jazzlene and Camille. Next thing I know in walks my 3yrs old baby sisters Serenity and AnnMarie in their white flower girl dresses dropping yellow/white rose petals on the aisle.

As soon as they saw me both bolted straight for their big brother. I scooped them up, giving them hugs and kisses before putting them down. I told them to go stand with Camille and be good girls for me. Serenity went and did as I said while AnnMarie went next to Ma. I took a deep breath and leaned over to my dad asking him was he this excited to see Ma on their wedding day as I am? To which he replied: I sure was son and still am everyday.

Right on time at 2pm out walked my bride arm and arm with her mother. The Full tulle ball gown, ruching in the bodice and a sweetheart neckline. Paired with a layered tulle cathedral veil was the most angelic sight. I couldn't stop myself from shedding a couple tears. After we joined hands Bro.Swanson began with a prayer over our marriage followed by the reading of Jer 29:6.

Bro.Swanson- Now Malcolm and Kapri have written their own vows. We'll let our Sis. Smith go first (he hands Kapri the mic).

Kapri- (In a shaky voice) Malcolm ever since the first day of class I wondered if you ever noticed me at all. Because like every female in our class I was thinking: wait til I get my hands on that man. The first time you took me on a date and told me you got all your dating advice from your parents. I thought I needed to hang out with his parents because this is the most fun I've had in my whole life. Once I met your physical and spiritual family I knew then that I'd found my future spouse. Your strength, character, charm and reassurance have made me stronger. Even the last 4 days here your texts put my mind and heart at rest. Here before all these witnesses I promise to let you lead our family and be your support. There's no man that can give me the amount of Love,Care,Compassion and Security that you have these last 3 yrs. I'm not only in Love with you but I am in Love with you.

Bro.Swanson-Those were some truly heartfelt words from our Sis.Smith now we'll hear from Bro.Williams.(hands him the mic)

Malcolm-(clears his throat) Kapri the day I approached you at school God told me you were meant for me. Every one of my actions in word and deed is a representation of him, not just of my dad. Just as you worried about me when I go to work everyday, I worry about you as well.

I always want you to know I Love You the same way God Loves You. Before all of these witnesses I promise to be your safe place of comfort and strength forever.

Bro.Swanson- Well at this moment by the power vested in me, I now pronounce you man and wife. Bro. Williams you may now kiss your lovely bride.

He didn't have to tell me twice because I've been waiting 4 ½ days to kiss this woman. I planted a kiss on my wife that brought everyone to tears except my little sisters. Everyone started laughing as Serenity and Ann Marie ran over and started pulling us apart. When I looked down at them my sisters were standing there with their lips puckered up for a kiss. So I gave both of them a soft peck on the cheek and they each gave me one as well. Kapri and I scooped both of them up and headed out to take pictures with the wedding party before the reception.

After the pictures were done my parents approached and offered to take my sisters inside so Kapri and I could have some alone time. They both had missed their nap time so I knew they'd be cranky but Serenity was determined to stay with her big brother. Kapri picked Serenity up and told my parents we'd keep with us until she settled down. After my parents went inside we took Serenity for a walk around the garden until she passed out then we went inside for the reception.

20

Great Reception

As we entered the castle for the reception Kapri handed a sleeping Serenity to my grandparents. Then she told me she needed to use the restroom before we walked in. 10 minutes later she reappeared in a Sophisticated fit and flare with a sheer bodice with beaded floral embroidered lace and keyhole back. I was definitely surprised when I thought she couldn't get more beautiful. She takes my breath away. Placing a hand over my heart I was even more in love with the Queen before me. Then I heard the DJ announce "everyone welcome Mr & Mrs Malcolm Rashad Williams.

When we stepped into the banquet hall I wasn't the only one speechless from Kapri's dress change. The guests and staff were also at a loss for words at how beautiful she looked. After everyone gave their speeches it was time for our first dance to which you say I'm quite the romantic(thanks dad). When the music started and the voice of Glenn Jones began to sing "We've only just begun" Kapri whispered that this was a favorite song of hers. Little did she know I chose all the music from all her playlists on her YouTube account. After our first dance I asked all the couples to join us on the dance floor for another dance.

Then the mellow sounds of Keith Washington & Chante Moore singing "I Love You" relaxed everyone. Every lady in the room was securely in the arms of the one she loved and loved her back. Then we sat down for dinner which was good even though Janette complained because TuTu Kane didn't cook it. With my mother-in-law making the wedding cake I asked her to choose the menu for dinner and she didn't disappoint.

Appetizers- Garden Salad, Corn & Black Bean Salad, Chicken /Beef Patties

Entrees- Honey Jerk Chicken, Orange Ginger Chicken, Asian Style Spareribs or Sweet & Sour Fish

Sides-Vegetable Fried Rice, Brown Sugar Crusted Plantains, Corn Pudding, Rice & Peas

Dessert-Citrus Cheesecake, Tropical Fruit Platter and Assorted Jamaican Pastries

After that hearty meal and the cutting of our cake all the kids went to bed. All the adults came back to the reception hall to dance the night away. When the staff started to clean up, that was my cue to slip away with my wife. Alone in the elevator heading to my suite Kapri kept repeating how this was the best day of her life. I couldn't take it anymore so I planted a kiss on my woman that made her forget those words.

The moment we stepped off the elevator my wife asked me which suite we'd be spending the night in. I already told yall which suite we're going into so off to the King Suite we go. She was so amazed at the size of this suite that she didn't want to touch anything in it. I took my lady by the hand and stood in the middle of the room. Before she could ask me a question I turned on the bluetooth and "Lately" by Tyrese came on and we danced again. Just holding this woman on our wedding night meant more to me than consummating our marriage.

When the song ended "Fire and Desire" came on Kapri looked at me like I was crazy. So I asked Alexa to change the song to "Can you stand the rain" which made my lady smile. As the song played she asked me to lay next to her in the bed and hold her. Y'all know I'll do anything for my lady tonight and every night after this one. We laid there listening to some of the greatest R&B music of the last 4 decades until we passed out.

By sunrise my dad had called saying that the family was packing up to head home. While my wife was asleep I got dressed and went to bid farewell to the fam. When I returned to the room a breakfast tray was waiting for us. As I walked into the suite Kapri was coming out of the bathroom looking radiant as usual. I was going to ask where you went but I see what you have in your hand, she said with a shy smile.

I sat the tray on the bed and told her the family wanted to say goodbye before leaving but she was asleep. Now let's eat so we can pack up and go on our honeymoon. I fed my Queen and headed for the airport. It was such a blessing to finally call the woman to my right **"Wife"** finally. Throughout the car ride to the airport I couldn't stop myself from repeatedly calling her **"Wife".**

21

Honeymoon Bliss

Once we made it to the airport our flight was delayed for an hour which was alright. In our first class seats everyone kept congratulating us on our marriage until lift off. Finally in the air we each had a glass of champagne and my wife gave me a

crash course in Jamaican culture. When we landed 4hrs 50mins later in Montego Bay, Janice met us at our terminal. We rode for another 20 minutes to Janice's home. The cozy 2 bedroom home felt just like home for me.

After we got settled in Janice was in the kitchen with Kapri making dinner. I sat on the porch watching the comings and goings of my surroundings. About 30 had passed when the ladies came out to get me for dinner. During dinner Janice informed me that she was going to make sure I see all the great sights of Montego Bay in one week. Ma, I just married him don't scare him off already, Kapri stated afraid. Baby you already told me on the plane that they won't like because I'm the Police so relax, I said jokingly. Enough about that you two get some rest and I'll see you in the morning, Janice said walking toward her room.

Day(1): After breakfast Janice dragged us out to the car and asked me to drive. I agreed to chauffeur my two pieces of precious cargo everyday. Where to Ma, I asked, putting the car into gear? We're going down by the beach where you two are going to have a Clear Kayak drone Photoshoot Experience. Then we're going Bamboo River Rafting and getting Limestone Foot Massages. I could tell looking in the rearview mirror that Janice was excited and out the corner of my eye Kapri was filled with joy.

Kapri gave me directions to our destination which took us 30 minutes to get to. We were surprised that we didn't have to wait in line since Janice had called ahead. Everyone kept congratulating us on our marriage during the activities. We stopped to get some food on our way back to the house. After showering and finishing our leftovers it was time for bed.

Day(2): We went Horseback Riding, Zip Lining and Tubing with the locals. My mother-in-law is just as cool as Ma, if not better. But don't tell Ma I said that though, I don't want to be on that woman's bad side.

Day(3): We had a sunset cruise but first we went ATVing through the hills. After lunch we went back to the house and took a swim. Once dinner was all cleaned up it was off to bed for everyone.

Day(4): We just chilled at the house with Janice and after lunch I went to the gym. When I returned from the gym the ladies were in the dining room having a discussion. So I made my way to the shower. After my shower I laid down for a rest when Kapri leaped excitedly into my arms. Babe, since we only have one more day here mom wants to take us to the club tonight. I'm down with that baby just wake me up when you ladies are ready,I said. After giving my wife a quick kiss I turned over to pick up my cell and call dad.

How's married life treating you son, my dad answered instead of saying Hello. It's treating me well and here I thought Janice was going to be like grandma but she's more like Ma than I expected. I haven't been able to call the last 3 days because Janice has been the best tour guide ever. I think she planned our whole honeymoon by herself and since tomorrow is our last day here she wants to take us to the club tonight.

That sounds good son, maybe we'll come down there as a group sometime, my dad replied. There are a lot of group activities we can do with the kids on the island too. Cool, bring your Ma some pamphlets so we can start planning for next year. I got you dad, I'll talk to you later. The girls are ready to leave for the club now.

Janice took us to Lounge 2727 which had a homestyle feel to it. The atmosphere was relaxed and we met up with some of the other tourists from the past 3 days. We ate with them and took a rum shot before parting ways. Then Janice took us to Taboo which is somewhere I'd love to bring the family on vacation. On my way to the bathroom I noticed an altercation about to take place and went to investigate. As I approached a young lady was saying "We need Police" and Janice out of nowhere yelled " My son-in-law is the Police".

Now everyone knows I'm a cop and decided to be on their best behavior. Once the situation was handled and the young lady involved was treated for minor injuries I turned to grab my ladies to leave. Then I was stopped by one of the officers asking if I really was married to one of their islanders? I nodded saying "Yes" then he extended his hand saying: if I Needed a job there was a spot for me on their force. I expressed my gratitude and then took my ladies home and have yet to get to the bathroom. Once we got to the house I made my way to the bathroom for much needed relief. Then I said goodnight to Janice and held my wife for a night of sweet dreams.

Day(5): Here we go on our last day with Janice but no need to be sad about it. Turns out Janice was headed back to Tennessee to house sit for us while we went to Hawaii. I went to the gym one last time before heading to the airport with the ladies. I called dad while I was at the gym informing him to have someone pick Janice up from the airport and take her to the house. At the airport Kapri and I thanked Janice for a great time and said we'd see her when we got home.

Once Janice boarded her flight it was time for us to board our flight to hang with TuTu Kane and TuTu Wahine. Once on the plane and after lift off we went straight into watching movies on Netflix. For the next 10 hrs and 49 minutes we were covered in peace and quiet.

When we landed there was a Lincoln town car waiting for us at our gate. The driver informed us that he was to bring us to my grandparents and let us take a taxi. We got in and took the 20 minute ride to the new home of TuTu Kane and TuTu Wahine. On the doorstep they stood looking like the image I envisioned for Kapri and myself. After we got settled in the house Kapri went into the kitchen with TuTu Wahine to cook dinner.

TuTu Kane sat with me in the living room to talk while we waited for dinner. I just had to ask him a couple of questions that I've already asked dad. (**1**) How did you know she was the one for you? (**2**) How do you guys keep the spark in your marriage? (**3**) How do you get through the rough days with TuTu Wahine?

He looked over at me and said son those are some good questions. First you know when you've met your match just by the way she responds to your presence in the room. Depending on how long you'll be staying will help me answer your second question. I told him we'd be there for 4 days so he said: we'll show you how we keep our relationship strong. Part of it is that we feel sorry for your PopPop dealing with Janette's comedic antics, he said with a laugh. I think the whole world feels sorry for PopPop everytime they're out together.

Lastly, son it's your job as her man to make her feel safe and secure everyday. If she's told you what she's endured growing up then you know what you're up against. My in-laws told me the whole story of what Marcus had done to her and your Ma. I made it my mission the first day we met to be gentle with her. I told her to be honest with me about her feelings so we could come up with a solution together. You never want her to be afraid of you or for you when you're apart. There are days when I watch Ramona from a far and see her fear and it tears me apart inside.

When she notices me and asks me why I'm so far from her? I ask her " Is it a bad thing for her secret admirer to live in his fantasy of her"?

Wow TuTu Kane that's smooth right there I'll try that sometime. Then the ladies called us for dinner and I could tell Kapri was proud of what they made us for dinner. Over dinner TuTu Wahine seemed just excited about us spending our honeymoon with them as Kapri and I were. After dinner Kapri helped with dishes before joining me in bed. Before closing her eyes she turned to me saying: I wonder what they have in store for us the next 4 days, don't you? I guess we'll be in for some surprises on our honeymoon baby, let's get some rest for now.

Day(1) After breakfast we went to The Big Island to visit the coffee farms. Kapri likes coffee. I don't, so this was for her and TuTu Wahine. Kapri found 7 different flavors she wanted to take home. As long as she's happy I'm happy. So I paid for them and we left to go on a helicopter ride tour. After the tour we had lunch at a local cafe and we had to explain to Kapri what she was eating and it made me happy that my wife was more receptive to the Hawaiian cuisine that grandma was before her wedding. But now grandma Janette thinks everyone should have Hawaiian food at their wedding and it has to be made by TuTu Kane.

When we got back to the house I called back home to talk to my parents. This time Ma answered the phone excited to hear from us and knowing we were with her parents made her even more happy. I talked to Ma for 30 minutes then asked where dad was and she told me he was out with Uncle Max and Uncle Rashad. I told Ma I was going to bed and would talk to them another time.

Day(2) This morning we went to the Cocoa Farm to sample the finest chocolate on the Island. Kapri wanted some to go with her Coffee so they packaged it for us and delivered it to the house.We even went snorkeling in Turtle Town. That was the most fun for me to do with TuTu Wahine and TuTu Kane. On the way back to the house Kapri got emotional, thanking them for all the fun activities.

When we walked into the house TuTu Wahine took Kapri into her room and closed the door. I asked TuTu Kane if he had any idea what they could be talking about? He replied:maybe she just needs some grandma time instead of a mom this time. when they reappeared Kapri was all smiles so I guess TuTu Kane was right. As usual I called home and this time I spoke to Camille because Ma was in the shower and dad was asleep.

Day(3) With one day left on our honeymoon what could they have in store for us today? Today we took the Ultimate Circle Island Tour. We even went to Waimea Falls as part of the tour. Before making our way back to the house we went on a Sunset Dinner Cruise. Man!!! That

Prime Rib dinner was the best meal ever for me. The air and water both smelled flavorful the whole 2 hrs we were out on the Harbour.

When we got back to the house everyone was ready for bed but y'all know I couldn't without calling home. Tonight Christian answered while playing his PS5 with Brandon. We talked about gaming together when I got home. Before hanging up I wanted to talk with my parents but Chris said they were out on a date. Just think one day that will be me and Kapri on dates leaving our children with a sitter mainly being Camille.

Day(4) On our final day here in Hawaii TuTu Kane and I hung out in the house. TuTu Wahine took Kapri out shopping for a few hours. When they returned we attended a Luau with a dinner buffet and show. As the sun set we made our way to the Fireworks Catamaran Cruise. At the start of the fireworks show every couple on that ship kissed and the staff cheered.

That was the biggest highlight of our whole trip for me personally. Just before we could get off the ship a staff member handed us a picture of our kiss. Kapri said she was going to frame it as soon as we got back to Tennessee. We made our way back to my grandparents home for our final night of sleep. I didn't bother to call home tonight. I was too tired to talk.

After a good rest it was time to spend a couple more hours with my grandparents. During breakfast TuTu Wahine asked if we planned on starting a family within the next year or so. The answer to your question, grandma, is "Yes, we plan to do that, " Kapri replied.

22

Returning to surprises

After a 9 hr 11 mins flight home we walked into our house to find my mother-in-law doing laundry. Upon noticing us she excitedly gave us hugs and said "we're going next door for dinner after you guys get settled. We slept on the plane so within 20 minutes we were ready to go to my parents home. As we entered PopPop was sitting in the living room with my dad talking about a case. After greeting them Kapri and Janice went into the kitchen with the ladies.

When dinner was ready we all sat down to eat and PopPop led us in prayer.

Dear Heavenly Father, we come before you asking for a blessing over this meal. We ask that you bless this newlywed couple joining us at your table. As your disciples we spread your word to all those who will listen. We ask these things in the name of your son, Jesus Christ Amen

Amen everyone replied in unison after the prayer then we started to dig in. About 10 mins into the meal Janette asked Kapri if something was wrong with her? I looked over concerned at my wife as to what could be wrong. My wife started to cry and I almost panicked. Then she announced **"We're having a baby"** and all the ladies ran over to hug us.

Then all my siblings ran over excited to congratulate us on the baby. I made a quick call to Harmony to give her the news about the baby. The whole time Janice and Ma were hugging and shouting "I'm gonna be a grandma". My dad and PopPop gave me a hug and congratulations on becoming a dad. I'm so nervous but excited about becoming a father. You know my dad is going to be the first person I go to for advice.

After all the excitement it was time to go home so my Queen could rest. A week later we put Janice on a plane back to Jamaica and I asked when Kapri found out we were expecting? Kapri said she was feeling a little queasy when we got home so she took a test.

A week later a letter came from the Men's Prison addressed to me from Jamal Reynolds. In his letter he asked how Serenity was doing and thanked me for being a part of her life while he was away. He also wanted me to know his release date is scheduled for March 25, 2026. My little sister will be 5 and starting Kindergarten by then. Y'all know big brother will be right there to see her off on her first day of school for the rest of her life.

At the end of the week Kapri had her first appointment with the doctor. Dr. Swanson let us know Kapri was 2 weeks along into the pregnancy. We should welcome our bundle of joy by February of 2025. After getting an ultrasound and some photos we went home happy on this day.

At this point now I'll stop talking to you guys and go hold my lady. Besides we have 7 months until my sister's wedding to a good guy that I trust. So, you guys can go hear my sister's side of the story regarding her bond with our expanding family. Somewhere in her story I'll pop in to let you know what's going on with Kapri, myself and our bundle of joy. For now,Peace

Message from the Author

Thank you for following the **Leaving Trauma Behind Series**. I hope you will enjoy the **Bonded by Love Series** following 3 of the 6 children shared between Zeek and Kahlani Williams.

Yours Truly, **K.Moore**

Don't miss out!

Visit the website below and you can sign up to receive emails whenever K.Moore publishes a new book. There's no charge and no obligation.

https://books2read.com/r/B-A-DOREB-SRKTD

BOOKS2READ

Connecting independent readers to independent writers.

Also by K.Moore

Bonded By Love
Bonded By Love (Malcolm)

Leaving Trauma Behind
Leaving Trauma Behind

Leaving Trauma Behind: Family Growing Pains
Family Growing Pains

Leaving Trauma Behind: The Golden Years
The Golden Years

Leaving Trauma Behind: Turning a new Leaf
Turning a new Leaf